Laura Charlotte

by KATHRYN O. GALBRAITH

illustrated by FLOYD COOPER

Penguin Putnam Books for Young Readers

Printed on recycled paper

Text copyright © 1990 by Kathryn O. Galbraith.
Illustrations copyright © 1990 by Floyd Cooper.
All rights reserved. This book, or parts thereof, may not be reproduced
in any form without permission in writing from the publisher.
A PaperStar Book, published in 1997 by Penguin Putnam Books
for Young Readers, 345 Hudson Street, New York, NY 10014.
PaperStar is a registered trademark of The Putnam Berkley Group, Inc.
The PaperStar logo is a trademark of The Putnam Berkley Group, Inc.
Originally published in 1990 by Philomel Books. Published
simultaneously in Canada. Printed in the United States of America.
Library of Congress Cataloging-in-Publication Data
Galbraith, Kathryn Osebold. Laura Charlotte/ by Kathryn Galbraith. p. cm.
Summary: A mother describes her love for a toy elephant she was
given as a child, a gift she has now passed on to her daughter.
[1. Toys—Fiction. 2. Elephants—Fiction. 3. Mothers and
daughters—Fiction] I. Cooper, Floyd, ill. II. Title,
PZ7.G1303Lau 1989 [E]88-9898 CIP AC
ISBN 0-698-11437-X
3 5 7 9 10 8 6 4

In memory of Mother
and to my dear friend Barbara
and once again to Steve
—K.O.G.

For my little one
—F.C.

Laura couldn't sleep. She tried but her eyes just wouldn't stay closed. Through the open window came the soft scent of lilacs and a slice of night sky. Were the stars out? She sat up to look.

"Are you still awake?" Mama whispered. "It's way past your bedtime."

"But I'm not sleepy," Laura said. "Tell me a story. Please?"

"What kind of a story?" Mama asked.

Laura pulled the covers up to her chin. "Tell me the story of Charlotte."

"But you already know that story." Mama sat down on the edge of the bed. "You've heard it a million times before."

"I know, but I want to hear it again," Laura said. "Start at the beginning. Start 'once upon a time when I was a little girl...'"

"Once upon a time," Mama began, "when I was a little girl, your grandma was in the kitchen making a cake—a very special cake—because it was my birthday, and I was five years old. It was going to be a tall chocolate cake with buttercream frosting."

"And pink sugar roses on top," Laura said. "Don't leave anything out."

"And pink sugar roses on top," Mama said. "Then the doorbell rang and Grandma went to answer it.

"'There's a present for you,' she called. 'For me?' I said. 'Something for me?' I ran to the door.

"There in the hall was a package wrapped in brown paper and tied with red string. Grandma used her scissors to cut the knots.

"Underneath was blue birthday paper and under the paper was a white box. And when I lifted the lid of the box—"

"There was Charlotte!" Laura cried.

"Yes, there she was. And your grandma said, 'Oh, what a beautiful elephant.' I couldn't say anything at all. She *was* beautiful. She had soft gray flannel ears and a long gray flannel trunk and a tiny, tiny flannel tail. Your great-grandmother had made her from the scraps of her sewing basket just for me.

" 'What are you going to call it?' your grandma asked.

"Charlotte,' I said. 'Her name is 'Charlotte.' "

"Because . . ." began Laura.

"Because I thought Charlotte was the prettiest name in the whole world," Mama said. "And from that day on Charlotte and I were best friends."

"Charlotte went riding in the wagon with me. We had picnics together in the garden and played school in the nursery when it rained.

"We shared afternoon naps and bedtime stories and sometimes even the flu."

"And at night we shared Ducky."

"Because Charlotte was afraid of the dark," Laura said.

"Ssssh, close your eyes," Mama whispered. "Yes, because Charlotte was afraid of the dark."

"Once," Mama said, "a terrible thing happened. Cousin Carrie came for a visit and we played hide-and-seek in the garden. But that night when I reached for Charlotte, she was gone! Where could she be?

"Had I left her outside, still hiding under the willow?"

"I tiptoed down the backstairs and peeked out the door.
The garden looked shaggy and dark. I shivered.

"Far, far away, past the lilacs and daylilies, stood the tall
willow. I was afraid to go out without Charlotte. Then I
thought, was Charlotte afraid without me?

"I pushed open the door and ran across the wet summer grass. And ran and ran until I ducked under the arms of the willow. There was Charlotte! I grabbed her up and hugged her. She was wet and—Oh!"

"I started to cry. Poor Charlotte had only one ear. Dinah, the cat, had chewed off the other."

"But it didn't matter," Laura said quickly. "Because you still loved her best."

Mama stroked Laura's hair. "No, it didn't matter. I still loved her best. And I sat right beside her while my grandmother sewed on a new flannel ear. We were both very brave."

"But one day I was too old to play with Charlotte. Instead of sharing picnics and tea parties, she slept on my pillow, safe on my bed."

"And then one day when I was older still, I carefully wrapped Charlotte up in blue tissue paper and put her away."

"For your own little girl," Laura said.

"For the little child I *hoped* I'd have," Mama said gently.

"Now comes the best part," Laura whispered.

"And then one day," Mama continued, "I did have my own little girl, and your daddy said, 'What shall we call her?'

"And I said, 'We'll call her Laura Charlotte. Laura after her grandma, and Charlotte because it's the prettiest name in the whole world.' "

"And then you gave Charlotte to me," Laura said.
"And now she's my best friend and plays with me."
   As Mama rubbed her back, Laura thought about Great-
Grandmother who made Charlotte from the gray flannel
scraps of her sewing basket.
   And Grandma who made the birthday cake and the
little girl Mama who ate it.

And now me, Laura thought. Circled by love, she
hugged Charlotte closer and closed her eyes.